Song of the Empty Bottles

New York 1968

Henry Z. Walck, Incorporated

Song of the Empty Bottles

by Osmond Molarsky

illustrated by

Tom Feelings

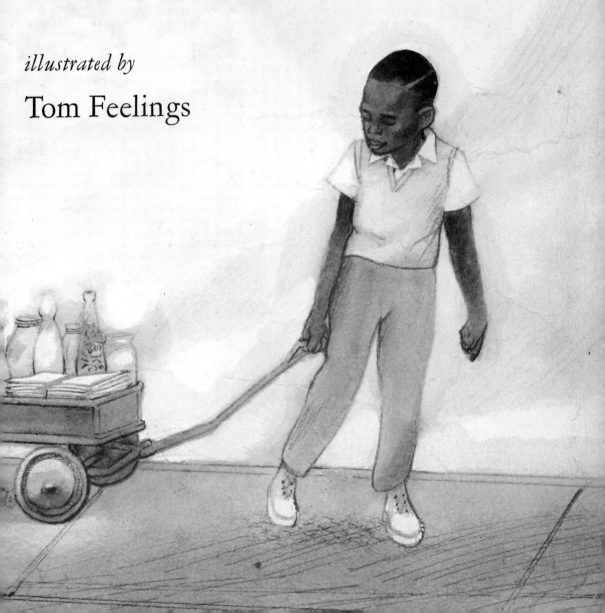

Thaddeus went to the Neighborhood House after
school whenever he felt like it—to make pictures
with crayons or finger paints, play ping-pong and
have fun. Some days he felt like it, and some days
he did not. But he never missed going on Thursday, because on that afternoon Mr. Andrews came
to sing songs with his guitar.

Some of the songs were happy and some were sad, and the children all sang along with Mr. Andrews—all but Thaddeus, who made his mouth go but did not sing out loud because he would rather listen. He did not want to miss hearing one single boom of Mr. Andrews' deep voice or a single pling-plung of his guitar. Instead, he waited until he was alone. Then he sang the songs, by himself.

Sometimes when he was singing, Thaddeus
thought of songs that he had never heard before.

My mamma goes away all day,
My mamma goes away all day,
My mamma goes away all day.

Then Thaddeus wished, more than he wished
for anything else in the world, that he had a guitar,
to make the wonderful pling-plung sounds to go
along with his singing, the way Mr. Andrews did.

One day when all the children were crowded around, Mr. Andrews said, "The boy in the back there. I don't think I know your name."

The other children looked around at Thaddeus and Thaddeus looked behind him, to see who Mr. Andrews was talking to.

"No. I mean you, young fellow. Come inside the circle. I want to talk to you." He was looking right at Thaddeus. "That's right. Come here."

Thaddeus felt hot and cold and frightened. He loved Mr. Andrews, but he had never dared go up and talk to him and lean against him, as some of the others did. But now the circle opened in front of him, and slowly he came near.

"What is your name?" Mr. Andrews asked.

Thaddeus put his head down and said in a soft voice, "Thaddeus."

"I didn't quite hear that," Mr. Andrews said.

"Thaddeus!" the other children screamed. "His name is Thaddeus!"

"I want to hear it from this young man himself," and Mr. Andrews put his arm around Thaddeus' shoulders.

Then Thaddeus spoke right up and said, "Thaddeus."

"Now will you tell me why you make believe you are singing in the back there, when you're really not singing at all?"

"I like to hear you sing," Thaddeus said. "And if I sing, then I can't hear you."

Mr. Andrews looked surprised and tried not to smile. "Well, I am flattered," he said. "But you would have fun singing along with the others, if you tried it."

"I have fun hearing. I sing when I'm by myself."

The other children were beginning to drift away, and after a while only Thaddeus was there with Mr. Andrews. Suddenly he reached out and touched the strings of Mr. Andrews' guitar.

"Here, hold it," Mr. Andrews said, and he put

the guitar in Thaddeus' arms in just the right way.
Thaddeus drew his thumb across the strings four
times. Each time he could feel the whole guitar
tremble in his arms, and he could hear the strings
ring in his ears like a million bells. He said very
softly, "How much is a guitar?"

"This one cost a great deal of money. A hundred dollars. Why do you want to know?"

"I want to have a guitar," Thaddeus said.

"But you don't know how to play one."

"I could learn."

Mr. Andrews looked hard at Thaddeus. At last he said, "I just happen to know someone who has a very nice guitar that he will sell for fifteen dollars. Do you suppose you could get fifteen dollars to buy it with?"

"I don't know," Thaddeus said, and he got up and walked quickly out of the Neighborhood House, straight up the hill and home, where he waited for his mother to come from work.

"What have you got inside you?" his little sister
Bernadine asked. Even when Thaddeus was only
sitting quietly on the front steps, his sister always
could tell when he had something on his mind.

"Nothing much," Thaddeus said.

"Tell me."

"I want to buy a guitar," he said.

"Will you let me play it?"

"Sometimes, if you're very careful."

"I'll be careful," Bernadine said.

After a while their mother came up the hill and turned in at the little iron gate. She sat down on the front steps to catch her breath.

"Have you children been good today?"

"Yes," Bernadine said. "Thaddeus wants to buy a guitar."

"A guitar! What do you want with a guitar?"

"I want to play it and sing with it."

"That's for big kids. You're too small to play a guitar."

"Can he?" Bernadine asked, following her mother into the house.

"Can he what?"

"Can he get a guitar?"

"How much is a guitar?"

"A hundred dollars," Thaddeus said.

"Are you out of your mind, boy?"

"But I can get one for fifteen dollars."

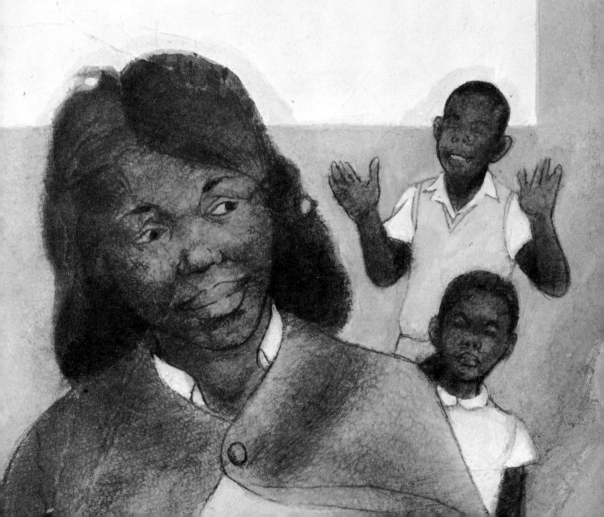

"Oh, that's different," his mother said. "No problem at all. You just go out in the yard and water the little banty tree every day for a week, and it will start growing dollar bills and quarters and dimes and nickles. Then you can pick them off and go downtown and buy anything you like. And while you're down there, would you mind buying me a dress and some shoes?"

Thaddeus knew that this was his mother's way of saying they did not have fifteen dollars for a guitar. Not right now. Or any other time, for that matter.

The next Thursday, after the story and singing time, Thaddeus waited to talk to Mr. Andrews. He told him how much he still wanted the guitar.

"Did you ever think of trying to earn some money?" Mr. Andrews asked.

"How could I earn some money?"

"Oh, I don't know. Running errands. Doing chores for people in your neighborhood."

"People in my neighborhood don't have any more money than my mamma," Thaddeus said. "They do their own chores and run their own errands."

"Yes," said Mr. Andrews. "Of course."

"I do earn money sometimes," Thaddeus said. "But only a little bit. Enough to buy an ice cream cone or a bottle of soda."

"How do you earn that money?"

"I collect empty bottles and take them back to the store. I collect old newspapers and take them to the shredding factory. They pay ten cents for a whole wagonload."

"Do you have a wagon?"

"An old rickety wagon," said Thaddeus.

"Well, if you collect enough wagonloads of old newspapers and find enough bottles, and if you don't spend the money for things to eat but save it all up, pretty soon you'll have enough to buy your guitar."

"How soon?"

"If you start right away, maybe you can earn the money by the Fourth of July—that's about three months."

"I wish it was July right now," said Thaddeus.

"Then you wouldn't have anything to look forward to."

"I would have the guitar."

"You win," said Mr. Andrews. "In the meantime, I'll teach you a little about how to play the guitar. We can use mine."

Mr. Andrews showed Thaddeus how to rest the guitar on his lap, with the fingers of his left hand pressing down on the strings and the fingers of his right hand plunking them. At first the strings cut into his fingers and hurt, and it was hard to remember where to put his fingers to get the sound he wanted. Often he made mistakes, and harsh sounds came from the strings. But he kept on trying, and every week, after the other children went home, Mr. Andrews gave him a lesson.

In time, Thaddeus learned six different ways to put his fingers down on the strings, to make six different chords. Each chord sounded different from all the others, and he loved every one of them. And no matter what note he sang, he could always find a chord on the guitar that made his song sound beautiful.

More than ever Thaddeus found himself making up songs, as he practiced on Mr. Andrews' guitar.

It's a hot day, Mr. Fireman.
Please open the fire hydrant for us.

It's a hot day, Mr. Fireman.
Please open the fire hydrant for us.

"That's a nice song," Mr. Andrews said when Thaddeus sang it. "Maybe someday you'll make up a longer one."

Thaddeus thought about that for a while. Then he said, "Yes, maybe I will."

Not as much fun as learning to play the guitar was collecting bottles and newspapers. No matter where he went, Thaddeus kept his eyes open for empty bottles. He found them in parking lots and in gutters and in trash cans. He found them in alleys and beside park benches. It was hard, slow work, and often he felt very discouraged.

But then Thaddeus discovered the tall apartment buildings that began a few blocks from his house. He heard that the people who lived in these buildings left their empty bottles in incinerator closets on every floor. They left old newspapers there too. He asked the building superintendents if he could have the bottles and newspapers. Some said he

couldn't, but some said he could. With his rickety wagon he carted the bottles to the grocery store, where he got refund money for them. He took the newspapers to the paper-shredding factory on the street behind his house. He collected every day after school and on Saturdays and Sundays, and he saved all the money he earned. He kept it in a peanut butter jar and didn't tell anyone about it, not even Bernadine.

Every few days, Thaddeus dumped his money
out on his bed to see how much he had. The pile of
nickles and dimes grew very slowly, and after eight
weeks he only had four dollars and seventy-one
cents—it would take him forever to save fifteen
dollars. But then he thought about the guitar, and
he put the money back in the peanut butter jar
and went out again to find more bottles and newspapers.

One Sunday afternoon he went, as usual, to the
Oxford House, which was ten stories tall. Every
Sunday, for the past eight weeks, he had taken the
elevator to the tenth floor and looked in the closet.

He would look in the closet on every floor, right
down to the ground. He did the same thing in all
the houses in the neighborhood.

This Sunday afternoon, the doorman at the
Oxford House wouldn't let him in. "Can't have
you in the building," he said.

Thaddeus left and went to the Cambridge House. The same thing happened there. "No boys allowed inside," the doorman said. "Go away."

It was the same at the Eaton House, the Rugby House, the Wiltshire Apartments and the Hampshire House. "Go away. No boys allowed." That was the story everywhere.

At the Embassy Gardens the doorman said, "Sorry, young fellow. Can't let you in."

"Why not?"

"There've been some robberies around here."

"Oh," said Thaddeus. "But I'm not a robber."

"I know you're not. All the same, those are my orders. Sorry." Then a lady came out and the doorman blew his whistle for a taxi, and Thaddeus went away.

The next Thursday, Thaddeus went to the Neighborhood House. At the end of the singing, he started to leave with the others, but Mr. Andrews stopped him. "Aren't you going to take your lesson today?"

"I don't feel like it," Thaddeus said.

"Why not?" said Mr. Andrews. "What's the matter?"

"Nothing much."

"Come on, now. Tell me. I want to know."

So Thaddeus said, "I can't get any more bottles from the apartment houses. They won't let me in. Now I don't think I can ever find enough bottles to save up fifteen dollars."

Mr. Andrews didn't say anything. He just strummed quietly on his guitar, and Thaddeus could see that he was thinking. Finally he said, "You don't care very much about collecting empty bottles, do you?"

"No, I don't care much about it at all."

"What do you like to do?" Mr. Andrews asked.

"I like to make songs and sing them."

"That's what I thought. But you've never really made up a whole song, have you? Like 'Blue Tail Fly' or 'Oh! Susanna.' "

"I guess not," said Thaddeus.

"Why don't you try?" said Mr. Andrews. "Whenever I hear a new song, I write it down. Then I can save it and sing it whenever I want to. Here's what I'll do. If you make up a song that I like, I'll pay you ten dollars for it. Then you will have enough money to buy the guitar and have a few dollars left over. Is that a bargain?"

Thaddeus could hardly believe it. Ten dollars for a song! It would take five hundred bottles to get ten dollars. And a ton of newspapers to get nine dollars.

A song was something you couldn't see or touch. How could it be worth ten dollars? Well, if Mr. Andrews said so, then it must be so. Thaddeus walked home thinking that he would make up a song that very night, after he went to bed.

Up until now, whenever Thaddeus made up a song, he did it without trying. It just came to him. He might be walking down the street and see something and make up a song about it. But, when he went to bed and tried to make up a song, no song came.

No matter how hard Thaddeus tried—day or night, walking, running, standing still or lying down—no new song came to him. What he thought, at first, was going to be a quick way of earning ten dollars was turning out to be very hard. Maybe collecting bottles was an easier way, after all.

And so, once again, he began to keep a sharp lookout for bottles. He had only collected a few when he suddenly realized that he was singing, making up a new song—a song about empty bottles. The words and the tune came to him in bits and pieces.

The first time was when he saw three bottles high on a wall. He had to wait for a tall boy to come along and get them down for him. "I saw three bottles on a high wall. I wished that I was six feet tall." Thaddeus thought maybe he could put that in a song.

Another time, he put nine bottles on the kitchen table and tapped them with a spoon. Each bottle made a different sound, and Thaddeus discovered that he could play a tune on them. This gave him an idea for still another verse. "I tapped some bottles with my spoon and got this funny little tune." Making up a song wasn't so hard, after all.

Then he remembered that the songs Mr. Andrews sang had a chorus that came after every verse. What could the chorus be? Thaddeus thought, "I can even find bottles in the dark," and then he thought, "That could be the chorus. 'Bottles in the alley, bottles in the park. If there is a bottle, I can find it in the dark.'"

As Thaddeus continued to look for bottles, he thought of more verses for his song. Some were good, and he remembered them and put them in. Others he decided were not as good, and he just forgot them.

At last, he thought that his song was long enough. When Thursday came, he took his money jar and went to the Neighborhood House. After the other children had gone, Thaddeus picked up Mr. Andrews' guitar and sang his song and played chords to go with it, to make his voice bounce and float along, high and sweet.

I look for bottles ev'rywhere,
Where I find them I don't care.

Bottles in the alley, bottles in the park,
If there is a bottle, I can find it in the dark.

I saw three bottles on a high wall,
I wished that I was six feet tall.

Bottles in the alley, bottles in the park,
If there is a bottle, I can find it in the dark.

I tapped some bottles with my spoon
And got this funny little tune.

Bottles in the alley, bottles in the park,
If there is a bottle, I can find it in the dark.

I saw a bottle in the lake,
Reached it with a big, long rake.

Bottles in the alley, bottles in the park,
If there is a bottle, I can find it in the dark.

After the first time, Mr. Andrews sang along with him on the chorus. Thaddeus could tell that Mr. Andrews liked the song, and he was not surprised. He liked the song himself.

Then Mr. Andrews asked Thaddeus to sing it again. He took out a pad and pencil and wrote down the words and drew some lines and marked down some notes. "All it needs now is a name," Mr. Andrews said. "What do you think of calling it 'The Empty Bottle Song'?"

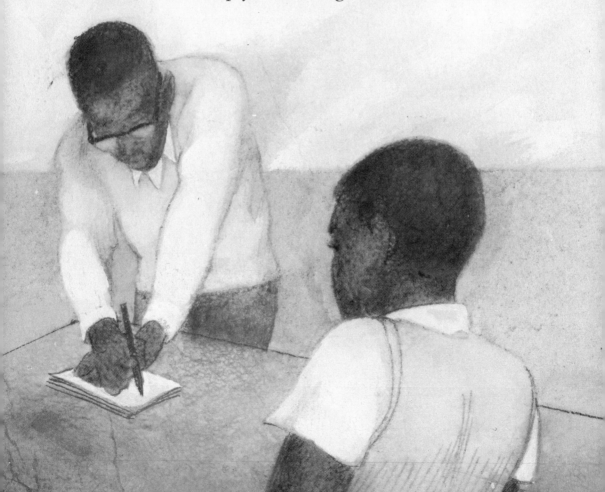

"I like that fine," Thaddeus said, and Mr. Andrews wrote it down.

"Thank you for the song," Mr. Andrews said. Then he took ten one-dollar bills out of his wallet and handed them to Thaddeus.

"Just a minute. The guitar is in my car," Mr. Andrews said, and he went outside.

Thaddeus emptied his jar of money on a chair, counted out five dollars and put it with the ten Mr. Andrews had given him.

Now Mr. Andrews brought the guitar in, handling it with great care, and polished it up a little with his handkerchief. Thaddeus could hardly wait to hold it. "Here's the fifteen dollars," he said.

"Thank you," said Mr. Andrews. "Here is your guitar," and he handed it to Thaddeus. How cool and smooth it felt, and it shone like a mirror. And when Thaddeus drew his right thumb softly across the strings, the guitar trembled. It was smaller and lighter than Mr. Andrews' guitar but just the right size for a boy. It did not have such a loud voice either, but it had a sweet voice. Thaddeus thought it was the sweetest sound he had ever heard.

Thaddeus carried his guitar home more carefully than he would carry half a dozen eggs. He walked fast but he didn't run, and he picked his feet up at curbs so he wouldn't trip. There, at last, was the iron gate to his yard, the scrawny little banty tree, the front stoop, the front door.

Thaddeus set his guitar down on the kitchen table. He got a glass of water and drank it, then got another and went out and poured it on the banty tree. How did he know? Maybe the poor little thing was thirsty.

Then he sat down on the front porch with his guitar and began to sing and play. He played "Blue Tail Fly," and he played "Oh! Susanna" and he played "Go Down Moses."

Pretty soon, people sitting in their windows and on their stoops across the street were singing along with him.

When Bernadine came home, she stopped outside the gate for just a minute, then came in and sat down next to her brother.

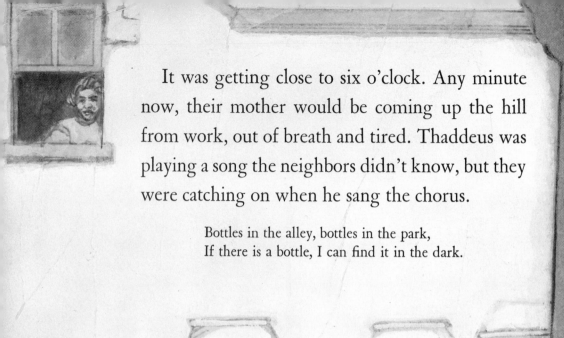

It was getting close to six o'clock. Any minute now, their mother would be coming up the hill from work, out of breath and tired. Thaddeus was playing a song the neighbors didn't know, but they were catching on when he sang the chorus.

Bottles in the alley, bottles in the park,
If there is a bottle, I can find it in the dark.

Thaddeus was singing a verse of the song as his mother reached the gate. She stood there listening.

> I saw a bottle in the lake,
> Reached it with a big, long rake.

Then everybody joined in.

> Bottles in the alley, bottles in the park,
> If there is a bottle, I can find it in the dark.

That was the end of the song, and Thaddeus' mother came through the gate.

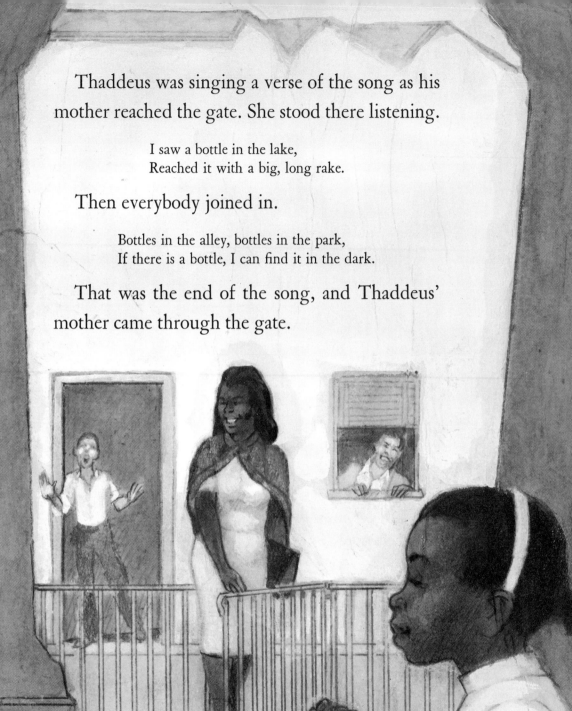

"What are we going to have for supper?" said Thaddeus.

"Son, I see you got that guitar, after all."

"Yes, Mamma."

"Where'd you get all that money to buy it?"

Thaddeus almost said, "I picked it off the little banty tree, Mamma." But he didn't say it. He said, "Some of it I earned collecting bottles and papers. And some of it Mr. Andrews paid me for making up a song."

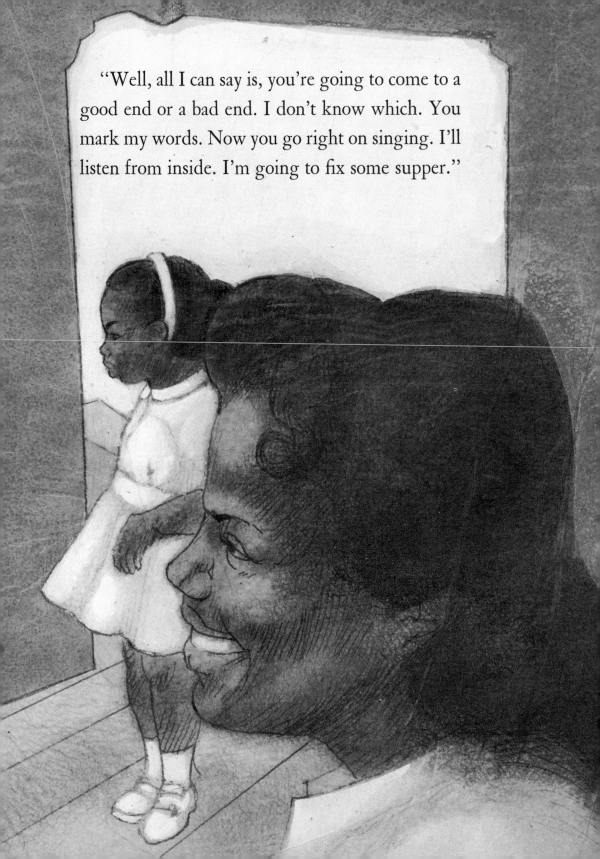

"Well, all I can say is, you're going to come to a good end or a bad end. I don't know which. You mark my words. Now you go right on singing. I'll listen from inside. I'm going to fix some supper."

Thaddeus drew his thumb over the strings three times and began to sing again. But this time it was a brand-new song. He had begun to smell the dinner his mother was cooking, and it was making him very hungry—so hungry that his new song was all about food.

Pancakes, cornflakes, squash and cherries,
Pickles, lemons, beans and berries.

This is the food I love to eat.
I don't care if it's sour or sweet.

Grapes and apples, bread and honey,
Stew and chicken, chocolate money.

This is the food I love to eat.
I don't care if it's sour or sweet.

His mother was calling him now. After dinner, he would make up more words for the new song. Then he could sing it for Mr. Andrews on Thursday.

THE EMPTY BOTTLE SONG

Moderate

I look for bot - tles ev - 'ry - where,

Where I find them I don't care.

Chorus

Bot - tles in the al - ley, Bot - tles in the

park, If there is a bot - tle I can

Last Time

D.C.

find it in the dark. Find it in the dark.

I saw three bottles on a high wall,
I wished that I was six feet tall.

I tapped some bottles with my spoon
And got this funny little tune.

I saw a bottle in the lake,
Reached it with a big, long rake.